WITHDRAWN

FLYING OVER BROOKLYN

For my mother, Sarah, who woke me with her kiss.
For my wife, Karen, for flying with me these many years.
For my beloved granddaughters, Alexandra and Kelli, their very own book.
—*M. U.*

To my wife, Morven, and with special thanks to Ross, Cherrie, Ruairidh, and Roisin.
—*G. F.*

CHILDRENS ROOM

Published by
PEACHTREE PUBLISHERS, LTD.
494 Armour Circle NE
Atlanta, Georgia 30324

www.peachtree-online.com

Text © 1999 by Myron Uhlberg
Jacket and interior illustrations © 1999 by Gerald Fitzgerald

Illustrations by Gerald Fitzgerald
Book design and composition by Loraine M. Balcsik

Manufactured in Singapore

10 9 8 7 6 5 4 3 2 1
First Edition

ISBN 1-56145-194-0

Library of Congress Cataloging-in-Publication Data

Uhlberg, Myron.
 Flying over Brooklyn / Myron Uhlberg : illustrated by Gerald
Fitzgerald. -- 1st ed.
  p.   cm.
 Summary: Lifted by the wind, a boy flies over snow-covered Brooklyn and admires its
winter beauty. Includes information about the 1947 Brooklyn snowstorm, the greatest in
its history.
 ISBN 1-56145-194-0
 [1. Brooklyn (New York, N.Y.) Fiction.   2. Snow Fiction.   3. Flight Fiction.]
I. Fitzgerald, Gerald, ill.   II. Title.
PZ7.U3257F1 1999
[E] -- dc21   99-26010
                        CIP

FLYING OVER BROOKLYN

Myron Uhlberg

Illustrations by
Gerald Fitzgerald

PEACHTREE
ATLANTA

When I was little, I lived in Brooklyn.
More than anything else, I wanted to fly.
I tried every day.

I flapped my arms...
I ran down hills...
I jumped from chairs...

Nothing worked, until one day.
It happened like this....

One winter morning, when deep drifts of snow
covered everything, I was sledding in the park.
The wind was blowing stronger than it had ever blown before.

I was trudging up the biggest hill when the wind grabbed my coat. I clutched my coattails. They were flapping like sails in the wind. (Mom had bought my coat two sizes too large—so I would "grow into it," she said.)

The wind blew even harder, and I rose right out of my footprints in the snow.
Slowly at first and then, as a fresh gust of wind billowed my coat,
I sailed up through the snowflakes into the great gray sky.

I wasn't afraid.

I wished my mom and dad could see me, floating high above our building. By leaning to one side or the other, I could steer.

Below were all the apartment houses, wearing snow caps and wrapped in white overcoats. In the streets, mounds of fresh snow outlined the cars buried underneath.

I could feel the snowflakes melting on my cheeks and the wind on my face. It made my eyes water as I held out my arms and flew slowly away.

All sound was muffled.

From high above I saw a smooth field of white with curved edges,
broken only by leafless trees standing in drifts up to their branches.
I knew where I was.

I swooped low over the lake in the middle of Prospect Park.
Somewhere, under all that snow, was the boathouse with
its swan boats.
I climbed up high again …

… and there was the Brooklyn
Bridge, its stone shoulders holding up a
web of steel arching over the frozen river.
  On the snow-heaped roadway, longer than five football
fields, all was still and silent. No chattering people hurried across the
expanse, no car horns blared, no screeching trains rushed along on silver rails.
  "Not just a bridge," my dad often said, "more like a dream." Looking down,
I understood what he was trying to tell me.

I circled back, and there in the distance was Ebbets Field, where Dad and I watched the Dodgers play baseball.

As I swooped low over the field I could almost hear
the sharp crack of the bat and smell the roasted peanuts
and the fat hot dogs smothered in thick mustard.

But the seats were buried in snow now, the wind
whistling through the empty stands.

And now, on to my favorite place in the whole wide world.

I wove swiftly around the snow-topped church spires,
taking care not to let my coat catch on their sharp points.
I was heading toward the ocean and…

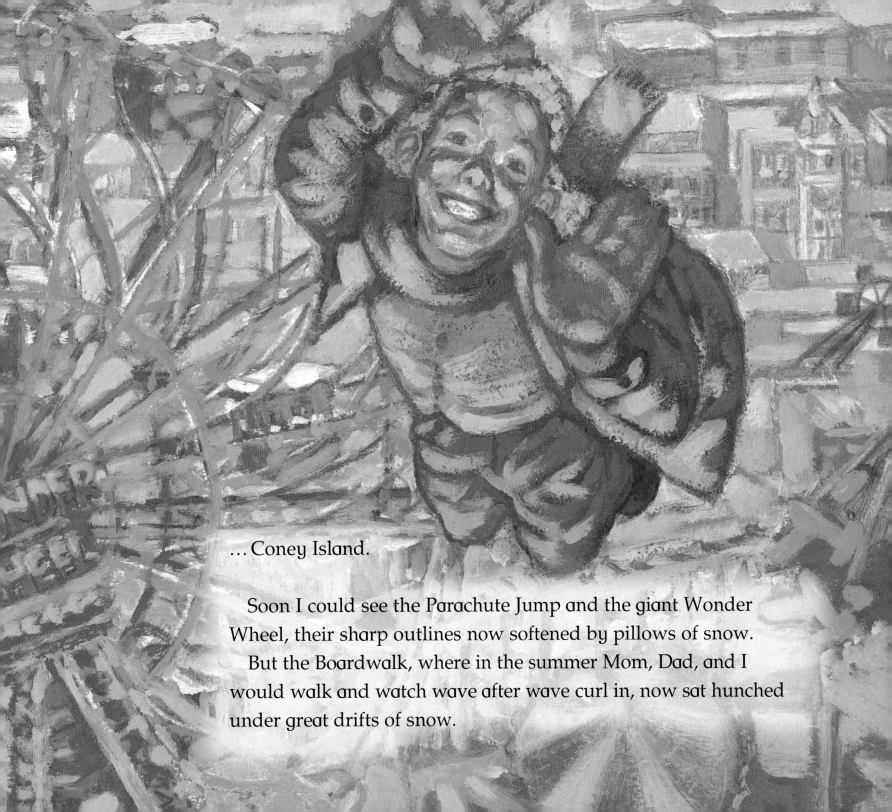

…Coney Island.

Soon I could see the Parachute Jump and the giant Wonder Wheel, their sharp outlines now softened by pillows of snow. But the Boardwalk, where in the summer Mom, Dad, and I would walk and watch wave after wave curl in, now sat hunched under great drifts of snow.

The Shoot-the-Chutes and the Cyclone were silent, without the cries and shrieks of summer riders.

The wedding cake towers of Luna Park rose up, the million electric lights now dark, each bulb topped with a tiny mitten of snow.

To the left was the Steeplechase Man, smiling on the snowy scene below.

The snow lay heavy over all of Coney Island.
Beneath the great blanket, I remembered
brightly painted wooden horses, their colors
shining in a thousand lights, leaping and
landing, galloping in an unbroken circle,
endlessly chasing each other's tail.

Buried were the ride tickets and empty soda
bottles, and my teddy bear that I lost last
summer, just waiting for me to find him again.

Summer echoes bounced around in my mind—the sounds of laughter and carousel organs, the cracks and pops from the shooting galleries, and the squeal of roller coaster wheels clattering down the rails.

I tasted again the sticky sweetness of cotton candy melting in my mouth. And I felt my mother's gentle touch as she wiped my face. She brushed the hair from my eyes and kissed my cheek.

As I turned my head
and opened my eyes, my
mother kissed me again.
"Come look out the
window," she said.

Author's Note

In the predawn darkness of December 26, 1947, snow began to fall over Brooklyn. The snow continued to fall, silently, relentlessly. During the next twelve hours, a record 25.8 inches of snow buried Brooklyn in drifts six to eight feet high, reaching windows and covering rooftops. It was then and remains the greatest snowfall in Brooklyn's history.

The author was a boy at the time. When he was awakened by his mother's kiss, he immediately knew something was very different. For although it was morning, his room was filled with a strange, pale gray light that cast no shadow, and he could hear no noise from the street below his window.

Normally at this hour, he would hear the jangle of the milkman's truck as the bottles rattled against each other in wire baskets, the barking of dogs, the shouts and chatter of neighbors and shopkeepers starting their day. But this morning he heard only silence, as if all the world were asleep.

Rushing to his bedroom window, he was astonished to see his neighborhood magically transformed into a world of absolute whiteness.

For the next several days he leapt off snowbanks and flew down hills on his sled.

And the memory of this wondrous event never faded.